little Miss Star

by Roger Hargreaves

WORLD INTERNATIONAL

Little Miss Star lived in Twinkle Cottage.

Now.

I'll tell you a secret.

You promise not to tell anyone else.

Don't you?

All her life, little Miss Star had dreamed of being famous.

She desperately wanted to be famous so that everyone would recognise her and ask her for her autograph, and she would have her photograph in all the papers.

But, she didn't know how.

She dreamed about it when she went to bed at night, and she dreamed about it when she woke up in the morning.

But, how could she become famous?

She had no idea!

Twinkle Cottage was just outside Tiddlyville, which is a small town a long way from where you live.

And even further from where I live!

One morning, little Miss Star was out shopping in Tiddlyville.

"Hello Miss Star," everybody called out to her as she walked down the street.

She was very popular.

But she wasn't famous!

And she wanted to be.

But, it was on that very same morning that little Miss Star had an idea.

An idea?

Not likely!

The Idea!

She was walking past one of the shops in Tiddlyville when something caught her eye.

She stopped.

And stared!

You see, it was that something that was to make her fame and fortune.

Would you like to know what it was?

I'll tell you later!

She jumped for joy.

And hugged herself with glee.

And she hurried home to Twinkle Cottage
as fast as ever her little legs would carry her.

She was going to be famous!

She knew it!

She ran upstairs and hastily packed
a suitcase.

Then she hurried downstairs, locked the front door of Twinkle Cottage and went to the bus stop.

The bus came, and she hopped on to it.

"Fares, please," said the driver.

"I want to go to Tiddlyport Airville," said little Miss Star excitedly.

The driver scratched his head.

"You don't by any chance mean Tiddlyville Airport?" he asked.

Little Miss Star nodded, and blushed.

The driver smiled, and gave her a ticket.

At the airport little Miss Star bought an airline ticket.

Where to?

I'll tell you later!

She had never been on an airliner before.

It was all very exciting!

"Hello," said an air hostess. "What's your name?"

"Little Miss Star," she said.

"And where are you going?" asked the hostess.

"I'm going," said little Miss Star, "to be famous!"

"Oh," said the hostess.

After the airliner had landed, little Miss Star collected her suitcase and took a taxi!

Where to?

I'll tell you now!

To a house!

The taxi drove up and little Miss Star got out.

She knocked at the door.

She could hear footsteps coming to the door, and then the door opened.

There, before her, stood a large man.

"Hello," he grinned. "Who are you?"

"I'm little Miss Star and I want to be famous!" she said, all in a rush.

"Oh you do, do you?" laughed the man.

"Well, you'd better come in, and I'll see what I can do to help."

Three weeks later little Miss Star, home again in Twinkle Cottage, just couldn't sleep for excitement.

"Tomorrow is the day," she thought to herself.

"Tomorrow I'll be famous!"

But she did get to sleep eventually, with a beautiful smile all over her face.

The early morning sun, streaming in through the bedroom window of Twinkle Cottage, woke her.

She jumped out of bed.

Little Miss Star was much too excited to eat breakfast.

She hurried into Tiddlyville.

She rushed up to one of the shops.

Which shop?

I'll tell you later!

The window blind of the shop was drawn.

So she waited.

And she waited.

And she waited some more!

But then, at nine o'clock on the dot, the window blind was raised and there, in the window, oh bliss!

She jumped for joy.

"I'm famous," she gasped.

And, do you know what was there, filling the whole of the window?

I'll tell you now!

Hundreds of books!

And, on the front cover of every book, there she was!

And there!

At the top!

In big bold letters, it said:

'LITTLE MISS
STAR'

"Oh me!" she gasped.

And there!

Underneath!

In colour, was a picture of herself!

"Oh my!" she gasped.

And there, inside, was her story!

LITTLE MISS STAR

by Roger Hargreaves

And here!
You are!
Reading it!

3 Great Offers For Mr Men Fans

1 FREE Door Hangers and Posters

In every Mr Men and Little Miss Book like this one you will find a special token. Collect 6 and we will send you either a brilliant Mr. Men or Little Miss poster and a Mr Men or Little Miss double sided, full colour, bedroom door hanger. Apply using the coupon overleaf, enclosing six tokens and a 50p coin for your choice of two items.

Egmont World tokens can be used towards any other Egmont World / World International token scheme promotions, in early learning and story / activity books.

Posters: Tick your preferred choice of either Mr Men ☐ or Little Miss ☐

Door Hangers: Choose from: Mr. Nosey & Mr Muddle ☐, Mr Greedy & Mr Lazy ☐, Mr Tickle & Mr Grumpy ☐, Mr Slow & Mr Busy ☐, Mr Messy & Mr Quiet ☐, Mr Perfect & Mr Forgetful ☐, Little Miss Fun & Little Miss Late ☐, Little Miss Helpful & Little Miss Tidy ☐, Little Miss Busy & Little Miss Brainy ☐, Little Miss Star & Little Miss Fun ☐. (Please tick)

ENTRANCE FEE 3 SAUSAGES

MR GREEDY

2 Mr Men Library Boxes

Keep your growing collection of Mr Men and Little Miss books in these superb library boxes. With an integral carrying handle and stay-closed fastener, these full colour, plastic boxes are fantastic. They are just £5.49 each including postage. Order overleaf.

3 Join The Club

To join the fantastic Mr Men & Little Miss Club, check out the page overleaf NOW!

Join Our Club!

MR.MEN & Little Miss CLUB

When you become a member of the fantastic Mr Men and Little Miss Club you'll receive a personal letter from Mr Happy and Little Miss Giggles, a club badge with your name, and a superb Welcome Pack (pictured below right).

You'll also get birthday and Christmas cards from the Mr Men and Little Misses, 2 newsletters crammed with special offers, privileges and news, and a copy of the 12 page Mr Men catalogue which includes great party ideas.

If it were on sale in the shops, the Welcome Pack alone might cost around £13. But a year's membership is just £9.99 (plus 73p postage) with a 14 day money-back guarantee if you are not delighted!

HOW TO APPLY To apply for any of these three great offers, ask an adult to complete the coupon below and send it with appropriate payment and tokens (where required) to: Mr Men Offers, PO Box 7, Manchester M19 2HD. Credit card orders for Club membership ONLY by telephone, please call: 01403 242727.

To be completed by an adult

❑ **1.** Please send a poster and door hanger as selected overleaf. I enclose six tokens and a 50p coin for post (coin not required if you are also taking up 2. or 3. below).

❑ **2.** Please send ___ Mr Men Library case(s) and ___ Little Miss Library case(s) at £5.49 each.

❑ **3.** Please enrol the following in the Mr Men & Little Miss Club at £10.72 (inc postage)

Fan's Name:_____Fan's Address:_____

_____Post Code:_____Date of birth:___/___/___

Your Name:_____Your Address:_____

_____

Post Code:_____Name of parent or guardian (if not you):_____

Total amount due: £_____ (£5.49 per Library Case, £10.72 per Club membership)

❑ I enclose a cheque or postal order payable to Egmont World Limited.

❑ Please charge my MasterCard / Visa account.

Card number:

Expiry Date: ____/____   Signature: _____

Data Protection Act: If you do **not** wish to receive other family offers from us or companies we recommend, please tick this box ❑. Offer applies to UK only